Samuel Bowles, Carolinn Edna Skinner Twing

Experiences of Samuel Bowles

Samuel Bowles, Carolinn Edna Skinner Twing

Experiences of Samuel Bowles

ISBN/EAN: 9783337336714

Printed in Europe, USA, Canada, Australia, Japan

Cover: Foto ©Raphael Reischuk / pixelio.de

More available books at **www.hansebooks.com**

EXPERIENCES

OF

SAMUEL BOWLES

LATE EDITOR OF THE SPRINGFIELD (MASS) REPUBLICAN
IN

SPIRIT LIFE,

OR LIFE AS HE NOW SEES IT FROM A SPIRITUAL
STAND POINT.

NEW EDITION WITH SUPPLEMENT.

CAROLINN E. S. TWING, MEDIUM.

91 SHERMAN ST., SPRINGFIELD, MASS.

STAR PUBLISHING COMPANY.

PRICE, 25 CENTS. POSTAGE 2 CENTS.

Experiences of Samuel Bowles in Spirit Life.

PAPER FIRST.

HIS ENTRANCE UPON SPIRIT LIFE.

As life faded out and I was gradually losing hold of the old body, what had before been an intense pain in my chest, slowly changed to a sensation of heaviness. There was no inclination to throw off the incubus that weighed me down. The sobs in the room and the low tones were like far-away murmurs.

My busy brain, in a few moments, brought up the vivid scenes of my life—its early struggles, its later successes—all were like a panorama, spread out before me. I knew that what had been called the "King of Terrors" was with me, but I felt no fear.

Gradually the scenes in the room receded far away. The efforts of the old form for breath seemed like some other person beside myself. And then the loved ones of my childhood days were around me, with bright faces, holding out their arms and beckoning me over. A sensation then came to me that I was rising up out of myself, and from right over the old head, there was another head that thought and saw !

As my spirit was withdrawn from the body, I could look down on the agonized face, and see the last efforts of the life principle in leaving it. There was no feeling of fear, no pain. Death is not painful. I can recollect now and know there was not even surprise. It was like some half-forgotten lesson that had come back to me with force : but there was no feeling of awe, such as I had often thought must come to the person facing the mystery of death.

I looked for a river—I saw none. I looked for the boatman, but I beheld only multitudes of glad faces as far as I could see. I had long before given up the thought that there were golden streets and gates of pearl, for I felt if there was an after life, it must be in accordance with nature. I tried to think, I tried to remember the many who were around me, yet they would say, "Not yet; rest, brother, rest."

And I did rest—such rest as only tired souls have who have just come out of the turmoil of earth life. I did not realize I was rising, and still I had risen to quite a height, for I remember looking back at the old home and the old body, peaceful, now, with hands resting—hands that would nevermore grasp the pen and wield it for my fellow-men. I think even then a feeling of regret rose in my heart as the ambitions of life appeared to have been cut off in their very prime: I sighed and said, " Dear old hands you have served me well, but your work is over."

" Yes, *their* work is over," said a voice beside me, "you have changed garments. Out of the old there has indeed been resurrected a new body that will take up the tangled thread of life where you laid it down and wield again a power over the children of earth that will be felt, and finish a work so nobly begun. Your work is not done: your active brain has worn out one body, therefore death is kinder than life, for every thought of beauty or power shall find its way back as though written in letters of fire! Therefore, brother, rest: but only to begin again with redoubled power!"

Almost unconsciously during this conversation had I been guided and helped into a room which had all the luxury, all the beauty of rooms in earth life; and each article was just as tangible to me as the articles in the old life. I looked at my hands and saw hands like the old ones, only every trace of age had passed away. I felt of my body, and found I was the same man, clothed as a man, with no difference, only the look of youth. Then again I thought of the old body and as by magic I could see down an inclined plane into the room where it lay, and I saw those who were performing the last sad offices.

I was then content, though I knew my loved ones wept. I could see an end to their weeping. I felt a pity for them, yet joy mingled in the cup, for with the clogs of earth life out of my way, with the strife all passed, a new ambition came to me, to be known yet in the old life, to do a work that should find its way if possible, even to the heart of a nation begun in purity, but made corrupt through greed of men: and I gloried that death was life, and a life that no circumstance or change could blot out.

I think I rested then; for a while all was a blank; but when I came back to myself, such a glorious view presented itself to me! I was not expecting to see the throne of God, but I saw Nature as never before : lofty mountains, winding rivers, lovely valleys where the green foliage made an arch overhead and left shaded walks; lakes with many a little boat, filled with pleasure parties; cottages, nestled down among green trees: mansions, that contained souls who had come up through great tribulation ; pavilions, beautifully decorated, made with open sides, where there is often a multitude of eager spirits, listening to words that come from the hearts of men and women who have' learned their lessons in earth life and have. risen through sorrow, but here have their place as teachers. All was peaceful : brotherly love was one of the conditions prevailing everywhere, as I saw it. I feel even now lost in wonder, when I realize that spirit life is so closely allied to earth life : that the heaven I had dreamed of is only your natural world intensified ; that nature without blemish exists for every soul; that personal life is so important that infinite wisdom has provided for it eternally ; that once a man or woman realizes an existence, they go on forever.

In my future papers, I shall try to show the relations of the two worlds, the advantage gained from entering here ripe, instead of in childhood ; the effect of war and bloodshed : the efforts of the spirit world to prevent great accidents, and its efficient work when they do occur; our manner of living : the food needed; what our sleep is like, etc., and most of all, the efforts of the Spiritual Congress to overcome the effects of the blunders made in the earthly one.

SAMUEL BOWLES.

PAPER SECOND.

MR. BOWLES ADVISES WOMAN TO EDUCATE HERSELF
AND BECOME A VOTER.

A spiritual life is only an outgrowth of earth life. Therefore, in order to have the most perfect thought, the most perfect powers of description, we ought to learn thoroughly the law of contrast.

On waking up more entirely to scenes around me, I could see that humanity in all its phases in coming over to the unknown, had only laid down its burdens to resume them again with a more intense ambition.

Instead of my individuality merging into and mingling with every other individuality, I stand out clear and distinct, a responsible being. That which in earth life I took upon my shoulders, either from a mistaken sense of duty, or engaged in because soul and honor were in it, is still my work.

Earth life is full of unfinished sentences and unpainted pictures. To the student, Nature is a fruitful field, and those who make her their chief study, laboring in practical ways to bring out from her great heart that which will supply the body without crippling the soul, are indeed on safe ground.

But to the man like myself, who has mingled with the great world, seen its grasping spirit, felt that the iron chains which bound Afric's sons—only one set of a series of chains that are binding lives even now: the revelations are wonderful !

While in earth life, I cautiously, from out of the
depths of political interest, threw out gleams to the
world, that the time might come when woman, who
is made responsible for the breaking of every law.
might have a hand in its making. Now, seeing the
great influence of womankind, I would say, without
shrinking, "Sisters, educate yourselves to the highest standpoint possible: leave fashion and its accom-
paniments of dissipation and recklessness in the
background, and see what must be done to save a
nation's honor."

Let there be no question of sex in voting ; but let
there be simply a standard of political education to
which all men and women must attain before they
shall be allowed the ballot. This is no hasty conclusion, and the fact that I did not give this thought
fully to the public in earth life, keeps my interests
more closely allied with earthly interests.

A wonder, born of disappointment, came to me when,
in traversing the beautiful walks of spirit life, I
could see men and women eagerly talking and de-
vising means whereby to accomplish these material
results, which I had supposed I had left forever behind.

"Ah! no," they said to me, "after the whirlpool of
journalistic labor, it would be impossible for you to
drop the old ambitions which are a part of your spirit as well as your earthly life. You have laid down the
pen only to resume it with an earnestness and power
never felt before; and while it will not in the least,
detract from your spiritual investigations, you must
go ahead, and from the old Principle, cautiously
evolve that degree of clearness and perfection to
which you were unable to attain while dragged

down by earthly cares and hampered by that great bugbear, Public Opinion."

True freedom has no fear, and though I shall not strike at men, I hope to strike to the corrupt heart of principles, founded only on the gain of the possessor.

You may ask, "How can our affairs on earth conflict with the affairs of the upper kingdom?"

I answer, if you would keep all of your people there, it would not; but so long as you are losing from your midst, men immersed in politics, women down-trodden and given so poor a chance in life, that some take refuge in the river, or anywhere to drown out the spark of life, because life was so cruel, just so long shall we study into the causes that are bringing the world or the nation down to one common basis of selfishness.

How many to-day, who are loud in praises of their particular favorite, have stopped in the whirl long enough to study the man they uphold? Because he represents a certain side, do the blind run wild in his praises, and say unto the ignorant and careless, he is the man. You may not believe me, but over here, wiser ones than I, say the time is not far distant, if the old flag keeps waving, when every person to whom power is to be given, must first give a certificate of clean hands and a pure heart.

They must show a past that shall give promise of a pure future. No feeling of self-aggrandizement will be allowed; but the places of trust, from the highest to the lowest, must be given to those whose hearts are daily aspiring to a higher life—to find wherein they can most nobly fulfil their duties. This we hope, from the knowledge we have here, is in no far-off future, but so near that its first premonition shall be felt, making its way to the great public heart this very Fall!

We are intensely in earnest in this, for much of the efficiency of spirit work depends upon the beginning made in earth life.

Who should feel it more than I, who laid my armor down only to resume it with greater force than ever? Our aim must be to strike at the very heart of corruption, and even I must not falter, if I have to bring to light the hidden means that are being used on both sides to place their favorites before the public.

From this unpleasant prospect, I turn with sickening and dread, and try to lose these thoughts in conversation with the high and holy minds who, through discipline on earth, have learnad wisdom. And when, in my eagerness, I would rush forth, determined to win—determined, with willing heart, to sacrifice my time, my present happiness, my all, to correct the great world's wrongs, such men as Theodore Parker, Judge Edmonds and others, will say, "Go slowly, brother; we too, when we came over here, at first, felt that almost single-handed we could bring about great results: that we could be venerated, loved and believed even as in earth life.

But we found that though the same same impulses of earth life, intensified, urged us on, yet to be known as of old, we must bridge the gulf, mankind has made between the two worlds." Orthodoxy, with unreasoning determination, would by one deadly blow, strike out of existence every record of the return of spirits, save that found in the Bible.

Strange contradiction, when the meaning of every church in the land should be—Is man immortal? If so, prepare for immortality. And from the greatest hights to the lowest depths, no answer can come save that embraced in Spiritualism! "

As I listened to these words, uttered with thrilling power, this thought came to me—To the great, bustling world, Samuel Bowles is dead! Kind hands have laid the old form away; loving hearts have caused to be twined wreathes, evergreen, to his memory: the words he has written will be thought of as the words of one dead ; and stronger than ever before came the resolution to live, not in the memory of old works, but in the doing of new ones ; and stronger than ever is my desire to show a world, struggling for gain and renown, of how little worth they are, save as they point to something higher.   I hope to show the followers of Christ that they follow him only a litle way.

They weaken the arm of a God who over nineteen hundred years ago, could make Moses and Elias appear on the Mount, and say this is not the day of miracles.   And it is not, nor ever was there a day of miracles.   For a God, a living Principle, inherent in everything, because he is a God of nature, would not step outside of nature to perform His work ; and by the same law that caused the man Jesus to be seen walking so far with two of his believers, now gives strength to spirits for a time, through the elements nature furnishes, to encase the material, and thus for a few moments converse with and be seen by the loved of yore.

Thus can a truly thoughtful mind weave link after

link of the old in most beautiful harmony with the
new. Remember that this fact of spirit-communica-
tion and spirit appearance, which seems so impossible now, is but throwing a new light on an old Gospel.   SAMUEL BOWLES.

PAPER THIRD.
MR. BOWLES FINDS HE HAD A WRONG IDEA OF HEAVEN.

My ideal heaven, the one I thought of in the long
hours when death and life were fighting for victory,
was one which changed the man—one which made
the avaricious man less avaricious: the liar one who
would immediately seek the truth: the drunkard one
who would wish to drink from pure fountains. But
a surprise awaited me.

In interviewing myself I found the same ambitions
existing, only much stronger. I found that to be,
was to retain the properties of self. Therefore, when
I first found the work that spirit life demanded, I
thought what a worse than myth was the old ideal
song, "There is rest for the weary." I turned aside
from the contemplation of the past, to see what new
resolves the future had in store for me. There are
times when the soul would soar upward; but to com-
plete perfect work, it must still review the past.

Advanced spirits tell me, when, at times, they
would look into the mystery of higher spheres, they
are called upon by a voice, not to be disregarded, to
visit earth life, and help free some suffering one
from the old body. So, when we would feel wise and

begin to know spirit life, are we called again to look into the old lessons of earth life. Thus, whatever comes'to us, we are not allowed to rise to that hight that the grevious suffering of one of earth-life's humblest children would not awaken our sympathy. The world is full of suffering, and a spirit to be cognizant of it all, must be omnipotent.

But with people of similar temperaments, there is a sympathy that, like a magnetic chord, draws the spirit to the sufferer. Our chief growth depends on how we receive the lessons that are taught us through our own suffering or our sympathy with the sufferings of others.

I do not wish to enter into personalities, but to deal with principles ; and though my heart is longing to reach in spirit, one mourning household, I must repress it all, and go on until there comes a time when hungry souls will be fed with the bread of life we can give them.

The days here are like unto your days ·there; but no night follows. Still, to every soul, there comes at times something like a silvery mist that is soothing and means rest. It comes when the spirit brain is tired and life begins to assume the weary feeling of the old life. Yet how great is the wisdom that causes these periods of rest as they are needed: for with the precision of the most perfect military encampment, each takes his stand, guarding those in earth life. This perfect order does not distress, and those who have been disciplined to it, never rebel.

It is a part of the great plan that the strong should care for the weak. When we see great

troubles hovering over you there, though we cannot
avert them, we can lighten their fall; and our greatest growth comes from the most efficient work done
to those who are still in the form.

The remark is often made in earth life, "I know
if my loved ones could come back, they would come
to me, not through another person." If you could
feel the grief it costs us to have such thoughts
thrown at us, you would not be so hasty in your
conclusions. Human nature and human loves are
selfish. There is not one spirit entering spirit life
but, if he had the power when he returned, undeveloped and without correct reasoning, would enter
his own home and on account of imperfect control,
would give terror where he meant to give peace.

Spirits in their first ardor would disorganize
families and bring again to you a worse lesson than
the Salem witchcraft. I know from my own long-
ings at first, how indiscreet we would be. So we
have to look at tears flowing that we cannot wipe
away, and at hearts aching, that we cannot cure:
and thus we settle down that the plan arranged by
wisdom greater than ours is right; that we must not
only have mediums on the spirit side through whom
we work, but mediums on the earth side, through
whom our mediums in spirit life work.

Thus there is a system which is right and just
for every one who would seek for communications
there, or for the one here who would communicate.

I shall in my letters, devote one to the subject
of the necessity for the best developed mediums, and
tell how to develop them, for many are needed, and

the more efficient work we do through earthly mediums, the more rapidly we advance here.

We do not count time here. Heaven has no Spring or gloomy November. Gradually, as is needed, our foliage drops, but in the old going down there is always the bud left for the new. Flowers that grow spontaneously, let the old stalks wither and out from the roots come the new.

It is not in nature that anything shall long exist in the same form; but out of the ashes of the old, Phœnix-like, shall come the new.

The duties of the household, which in earth life cause such hard work and aching feet, are performed without much manual labor in a way to satisfy every want. Everything moves with regularity. There is no clashing here, in a well-developed household.

The sympathy between the two worlds is so great that when you are supplying your bodily wants by cooking, we get the spirit of the food which rises, and it is utilized by us; and as our appetites are, such food do we attract to us. I hope I may be understood in this, for I have seen gluttons in earth life who shrank from death because they feared they would have nothing to eat. Many sad experiences come of these appetites. Not long ago I was sent with an anxious mother, to help guard her son and if possible, break a spell which was over him.

As quickly as the wind, the mother went to her boy. We found him near one of earth's foul dens where poison is dealt out and the dealer laughs at his victims. But on nearing the boy of seventeen years, the mother's face was clouded, for, coiling around him like a deadly serpent, was the spirit of one who had lately come over with delirium tremens, gloating and rejoicing that through this innocent victim he could for a brief time enjoy the old vice.

Could the mother or I break that spell? No—not then. Though good should crush out evil, we were too late. This spirit, before he could be disciplined must have that one backward glance; and the boy, with his negative disposition, must have that one experience, that the mother heart might, through his remorse, get a firmer hold.

Sometimes I think, if I had the Infinite's or He one half of my love, I would revolutionize the whole plan of earth and heaven; and then, when I see how, after a time, even from out of the depths, there works out a perfection, grand and beautiful, I try to be content.

If we could teach the children of earth life to avoid bad companionship, it would be a great thing; but if we could go farther, and protect them from the subtle influences of spirits who are in a hell of their own making, it would be better still. ' ' '

May angels help me to teach you on earth the true law of protection.

SAMUEL BOWLES.

PAPER FOURTH.

THE CRIME OF LEGALIZED MURDER. ITS EFFECTS
IN SPIRIT LIFE.

To a practical mind, one who looks into the soul
of things, the first years in spirit life are a succes-
sion of surprises. I have asked to be shown the
spiritual in all its phases. I have voluntarily left
the abodes of peace to look upon the wonderful variety of experiences to which those in our life are
subject; and if we over here could, with one mighty
stroke, wipe out some of the conditions of earth life,
we would do it.

A feeling of shame comes to me that
when earth life was mine, I did not more persistent-
ly work to help banish from the national government
that crime of all crimes "legalized murder!" Can
not you see that the old law of an "eye for an eye
and a tooth for a tooth," should have been left in the
barbarous past? A company of seven were sent
not long ago, to your world to help over the spirit
of a murderer. He was guilty of the crime. His
hands were red with the blood of his victim. The
deed was done under the influence of liquor. The
brain was maddened by jealousy. He was poor.
He had no counsel except what the state provided.

A man's guilt or innocence depends much, with
the great world upon the state of his pocket. The
"extenuating circumstances" often for criminals,
mean money. This man had not even friends. It
is true, a woman had been the cause of trouble, but
idle words had increased it. The culprit must be

hanged. Children must be made fatherless–the wife a widow. The look on that man's face, as he was led out with the usual accompaniment of officers and clergy, was fiendish. Not a thought of sorrow for the deed came to his soul. The prayer of the "man of God" was answered by a curse.

Men, many and of all ages, had gathered to see the slaughter of a human being. Oh! wicked world that gloats on misery! The sheriff, a fair-faced blue-eyed man, and a Christian, put his foot to the machinery that did its dreadful work, and an immortal soul had passed the boundaries. The sheriff was complimented on his coolness: the priest said, "God have mercy on his soul:" and another unripe spirit had come to us to learn new lessons,

"What will you do with him now?", I asked, as I saw a weeping mother, trying to catch one glance of recognition from him. Sadly came the answer, "he did not live out his time there, his spirit must still stay on the earth plane until the time when nature would have released him."

There was not even a feeling of gladness visible on his face that he could see those he called dead. Though gentle hands were held out to him, though kindly words were spoken, he heeded them not; his soul was thirsting for revenge—on the jury who found him guilty—on the judge who sentenced him, and most of all, on the sheriff who hung him, was his mind made up to seek revenge.

"What will be the result of this act?" said I to Judge Edmonds.

"The same as of many of the others," he sadly

said. "One murder paves the way for many others: he has murdered one man, the sheriff has murdered him, and now with a desperation not known in earth life, will he obsess some negative person, and blindly, madly exult in taking some life."

The decree has gone forth, and until the spirit of good can by degrees, banish the spirit of evil, the fatal work will go on: and if as I hope, this little book shall find its way to many households, angels grant it may awaken in the children of earth, a desire to expunge from the laws of a great nation, the law of a life for a life.

If the glance of judge and sheriff shall rest on these pages, may it awaken in their hearts the feeling that they too are murderers, for they take a life they cannot give. If, instead of the money of states or countries being used for such prolonged trials, those who were really known to be guilty, were put in clean, comfortable places where the soul could grow and their hands always be employed in work which would bring money to the state, it would be far better. It is a wrong idea that it would increase crime.

The dread of death is not half as strong in most hearts as the dread of an imprisoned life. Not only would this system give a purer look on the nation's page, but it would help heaven. It would lessen the number of murders in earth life. It would give to every man and woman a chance for self-improvement, even though on the lowest round of the ladder. It would inspire noble resolves, and give a chance for purification. O! world of struggling mortals, see you not you are weak when you should be strong!

Those who, from this side, watch the affairs of state, feel that the spirit world must do its best work on the active law-makers in earth life, to try to remove this great evil, which, like a moral malaria, has fastened itself upon the minds of the people.

Men who deem their robes are spotless will find over here that they are stained with a brother's blood.

Let this work go on. Correct this evil, and heaven's inhabitants will rejoice that one more step is taken up the "golden stairway."

SAMUEL BOWLES.

PAPER FIFTH.

THE CRIME OF UNLEGALIZED MURDER.

THE EFFECTS ON THE SPIRITS OF CHILDREN, SENT TO SPIRIT LIFE BY ABORTIONS. HOW THE DOCTORS WHO PRODUCE THEM ARE TO BE DAMNED!

As I intend to deal with the facts of earth life, and leave the fancies to others, I will now, after treating of "legalized murder," write of murder which is carried to such a wide extent among the denizens of earth. Had I not seen its direful effects in so many cases, I would not risk shocking an over-sensitive world by the knowledge of what is daily passing before them; yet with closed eyes they allow manifold transgressions to pass by—transgressions in broad-cloth and in silks and satins.

Men and women, either from the love of ease, or

money, wish to cover up one sin by the doing of another. So countless souls are ushered into eternity without even the experience of being born into earth life. A man who would be hung should he murder a child six weeks old, with the greatest carelessness, murders a child six or eight weeks after the decree has gone forth that another soul shall develop a body with which to meet the experience of earth life. And thus the sin goes on. Mothers in fashionable life shrink from that which nature demands, and without thinking of refraining from the cause, destroy the result. They not only exult that they have again become free, but they plunge all the more deeply into the dissipations and wickedness of earth life and like the miller, flitting around the deadly flame, soon destroy self.

Competent physicians inform me that each abortion means five years less of life to the mother; and once she has permitted the deadly sin to occur, she puts her physical system in ten times the peril of natural childbirth. This must needs be so, as it is an outrage on the physical, and a dragging down of the spiritual. It not only destroys the body of the child, but it so dwarfs the natural growth of its soul that many years will be required to get it into line again.

Wealth destroys children to shirk the responsibilities of life; and poverty destroys them, often innocently and from the force of circumstances. The over-crowded dwellings of the poor, seem to teach no lessons to the masses. If a child is gestated and born, under the best conditions once in five years, it is all that is right for a father or mother to endure.

Allowing the passions to have full sway, even in married life, is a deadly sin, because it sinks humanity lower than the brutes. It disorganizes society, makes the woman flee from her husband, and brings to life dwarfed bodies and dwarfed mentalities. I hope I do not put it too strong when I say that at least one third of the children born in earth life are the result, not of earnest prayer to reproduce the likeness of a loved object, but simply of an over-excited imagination and uncontrolled passions.

Therefore, these children have inherent in their very beings, the results of a past when they were helpless, and they must suffer for every one of the diseases and passions implanted in them. Children that come unwelcome, with the daily wish in the mother's heart that she should be freed from her burden, often inherit such a passion for murder as almost amounts to a mania. The Pomeroy boy murderer is as innocent in himself as an angel. The mother during pregnancy was forced by a brutal husband to help hold the quivering animals after he had dealt the death blow. The contact of hands, the anguish of the creatures were all so pictured on her mind, that she brought forth one who exulted in agony and death. Surely the sin and ignorance of one generation shall descend to another. That boy's name has been sounded all over the world, while he is innocent. The child victims who fell under his hands, were the outgrowth of a cause which must go on until, like troubled waters, their very motion and existence will create purity.

Mothers, all over the land, who claim to love your children, do think of the blasted lives you have sent into spirit life unasked, and with only the tiny germs of development that you either in wickedness or ignorance, gave to them. Can you wonder that even angels are not strong enough to take the little lives which must begin in impurity and clear all the weeds out of their hearts? No, the undeveloped one must seek in earth life and from its natural protectors or from others, the strength to grow in spirit life.

Therefore, when they visit the mother and find no love in her heart, it engenders intense hatred. It often calls out the worst in their natures, and makes them attach themselves to negative persons who will brave temptation for awhile and then succumb. There are places here where such little infants are kept in darkness and quiet until the time when they should have been born, and loving, attendant spirits try to quench the spark of hatred and make pure souls of them. But as soon as these dwarfed spirits are free to act for themselves they as naturally gravitate, in most instances, to the very gutters of earth life, as the moth does to the candle.

So doctors in broadcloth, bought with the money you have obtained for committing the dastardly crime; so women, who have transformed yourselves into fiends by that murderous practice, stop and think whether it will pay—for every child forced into the spirit world by your hands, will be demanded years and years of reparation. A hell is as necessary as a heaven, and you cannot help but suffer from the outgrowth of your own wrongs.

Men, who make laws, you have indeed been lax in enforcing them. The mighty dollar is all-potent, and sometimes I fear will close the mouth of the most powerful officer of the law.

What a mockery! Right before your eyes in this city (Springfield, Mass.) are daily sold drugs, and are often performed operations that are like throwing pebbles into the sea, making enlarged circles of wrong, which will go on for many years.

What are you thinking of? Can you afford to turn the tide of your lives into the swift channels of wickedness and misery? The world will move on, but if I could make you stop and think, and have the thinking result in a better growth, I should feel more honor came of it than to be the ruler of a kingdom.   SAMUEL BOWLES.

PAPER SIXTH.
LIFE'S BILLS OF SALE.

I have hesitated much as to what ought to come in direct line with my later papers, but I feel I must touch on ground which my happy home life there, and the multitudinous work before me, scarce gave me cause or time for serious forethought.

But as I have written of "legalized murders" and "unlegalized murders,! I feel it might not be amiss to touch upon, with ungloved fingers, the cause in some degree, of all the filth and wickedness of earth life.

I have looked into faces here that bore the marks of a wicked life. I have heard history after history of "life's bills of sale," where, because there was wealth and glitter, because there were stately mansions and costly equipages, because the parent in his seeming wealth was sometimes the slave of the wooer, because a daughter was sometimes willing to be sacrificed to a father's necessities, the hand is often given when the heart is not quickened by one thought of love for the man who would soon become her owner. I hope I do not put it too strong—was she not bought with a price? But the sacrifice must go on. Fashion, mighty in its reign, must be satisfied. The confusion, congratulations, hasty journey, may bring a glow to the cheek and people may envy her high position; but after all, if ever "bill of sale" was made out for one of Afric's sons, that woman has sold out all that was available of self.

But all was not available. A feeling of satisfaction may be felt that she has done so well (as the world counts it) and helped her parents out of dificulties, but there is not a woman's heart in all the earth but has, hidden away in its secret depths, an "ideal" pure and holy; and though often in these sacrifices she does not feel she has ever seen the real counterpart of her nature, there is danger every day that the depths of her soul may be stirred by this new realization.

But time goes on. The woman, finding nothing

to satisfy in the home relation, plunges into fashion's vortex. The pale cheek grows paler, and commingled with her life there may be another life struggling for existence. The struggle is unequal. No pictures of joy for the future rise to that woman's heart. Strange hands, working only for the means that their care of it will bring, will administer every thing to lessen trouble and keep it quiet.

Unnatural food may do the rest, and the child comes over here undeveloped, with but few elements in itself whereon the spirit world can work, and give it the needed spiritual growth. Or, if the chain of its earthly existence shall have been snapped before the time for its entrance into earth life, and its little life cast out into the great sea of eternity, the best that can be done cannot soon mend the broken links of its being, and it must of necessity remain long an undeveloped spirit here.

You there, wonder why spirits should ever be untruthful; because the word spirit should signify purity. Send over pure spirits and less dwarfs.

Beside the very carriage of the person we have pictured, may be seen a shop girl, fair in form and feature, but bearing the imprint of poverty. The best she can do, she can only pay for some wretched room and the plainest food and raiment. But she is told that she cannot appear before their class of customers until she dresses better. These words may mark the way for an immortal soul.

Temptation is waiting outside. A smile will almost buy her a dress, and one week's compliance in dishonor give her more real gain than a year of the strictest economy. The more she sins the easier it comes to sin. Little lives started in infamy are sent to us. The weary soul will always find her sisters ready to hold their skirts far away as if to escape contagion, while the one who made her thus is welcomed into the first society. Mothers lay snares for their daughters' benefit, while his victims are suffering, mayhap, keen remorse ; and he who is tenfold more guilty, has a grand palace in the great world.

Who is the prostitute? Who, in the sight of heaven is most guilty ; the one who sells herself for a place in the world of fashion, or she who sees starvation or crime before her ?

I am thankful that there are better avenues opening for woman, and that the chance will be given if she wishes to be pure, she may be. But the whole social relationship of the world is on a wrong basis, and to change it to anything like harmonious relations, or the chance for them, would be to disorganize society, and make for a time, a chaos of affairs.

Yet we in spirit life shall work, not only for your happiness there, but to make happier the first entrance into spirit life.

The world is like the rivers and smaller streams, all making their way to the great sea ; and so the motley crowd are coming, one by one or in great numbers, into this ocean of eternity.

The work of reform should begin when the germ is developing. The mother, if she sees the great mistake of her life, must throw upon the unborn, thoughts of beauty and purity. Nor does the work end with the mother. When fathers learn the great law of ante-natal conditions, they must work for the perfection of the human embryo much more faithfully than for its amusement and support when it is a living, self-existent soul.

With what ardor does a man devote his mind to the perfecting of fancy stock, while often times he allows his wife to be overworked at the time she is preparing to make him father of an immortal soul. Men and women, stop and think! Pay as much attention to the mother as to the animals in your barns.

When people are born right, when children are instructed that the most perfect and necessary elements of their being must be kept pure and holy for the reproduction of the race—when children are taught these things in the safe precincts of home. and not allowed to learn them on the street ; when the most beautiful and grand of nature's works shall be talked of sensibly and unblushingly, and not degraded by a vile imagination—then will be thrown into this troubled pool something that shall purify it completely.

That does not sound like Sam. Bowles, will be said by many lips, and I will say it is not said by the Bowles whose life was so intermingled in the chaotic sea of party and politics, but by the thinking Sam. Bowles, who knows that if politics or any other essential of the great world is ever made pure, it must be so by striking at the roots of existent evils. and not by pecking gingerly at the little twigs whose growth is only strengthened by the slight pruning.   SAMUEL BOWLES.

PAPER SEVENTH.

THE EFFECTS OF WAR AND SUDDEN DEATH BY ACCIDENT ON PEOPLE ENTERING SPIRIT LIFE.

It is often said in your world, if spirits possess a superior knowledge, why cannot they prevent some of these blood-curdling accidents that, at one stroke, usher hundreds into eternity? I will try to give you what light I have received on this question.

We can see the cause which is to produce an effect long before you can, because our brain-power is more subtle, our power of locomotion more rapid, and the thousand ills attached to earthly bodies affect the spirit but slightly. Therefore, had there been in the late accidents anything premeditated, and the thought of their being brought about been in any one's brain, the friends over here of those who would be in most danger would, and could have, were a medium available, prevented such accidents ; or had there been a seeming increase of carelessness that might in the near future produce the effect, that also could have been prevented, were the right sensitives within our control. But, so far as my observation has extended, we, spirits govern the spirit of prophecy only so far as, by virtue of our interest for our loved ones, we are able to perceive the cloud, not so large as a man's hand, that shall at last burst over their heads.

An experienced spirit-physician can fortell death in the most natural way. Added to the knowledge of the human is the clear sightedness which renders it possible for his practiced eye, not to gaze at the outer, but to look through the frame, seeing the tendency and calculating how long it will take that cause to produce the effect of a change of body.

The years I have spent in my spirit body are beginning in a measure, to teach me the possibilities of myself; and my field of study is broad as the universe.

We converse with each other when told of some accident which has brought its victims over. When there are many coming there is no confusion. Those most competent are delegated by that order which is heaven's first law, to assist the spirit-relatives to help their earth-friends over; for in our life as well as in yours, emotions move the soul and those really competent to help loosen the the cord of life in others, when it comes to their own, are made incompetent by their own emotions, unless much experienced.

At all places where horrors are many, spirits from the upper grades of spirit life work with as much ardor to help the unfortunate as though the ties of blood were strong between them.

This subject of accidents and war, and their effects on those coming through them to spirit life,, is a broad one. How often in earth life I used to hear people say, "Thank God, he was killed instantly; he did not suffer in the least!" And I thought it almost a death to be envied. But now that I have learned something of the mission of suffering, I see the natural way is far better, that is, to change by disease which ends in death.

Nature is a mighty sovereign. She will not be cheated one iota out of her work. She is all powerful, and therefore, on the mighty battle-ground where hundreds of men fall, changed in a few moments to the spiritual, the first movement of the spirit is to reach for the deadly weapon which was in his earthly hand. Murder, war and bloodshed are still rife in his soul. The kindly faces bent above him are, to his disturbed imagination, the faces of the enemy. The far-off din of battle wakens in him, fight.

It is very hard, at times to convince them that they are in spirit life. The shock to the body, taken over in any sudden way, shocks the spirit—more so when anger is in the heart, or ambition to be brave in battle, than when unexpected accidents bring them over.

They have lacked some of the experiences of earth life, which they should have had; and therefore. they are to make up for that through slower growth

Thus, under the great, blue canopy of spirit life, there are hospitals for sick souls, the same as in earth life there are for sick bodies. Warm hearts sympathize with them; friendly hands show them how to manage the new form. They are led to their old homes, taught the way to return whenever the telegraphic chord of love draws tham downward ; and as they grow stronger and their tastes for new light are developed, those who loved them in earth life, but have been here longer, gradually show them that they can enter into heavenly joys and be content to rise. Thus do they at length assume the duties of the new life, and throw off from them the effects of being robbed of that which should be the possession of every soul—the chance to ripen to the best possible degree on earth before being ushered into the experiences of spirit life.   SAMUEL BOWLES.

— -   ...   —

PAPER EIGHTH.

HEAVEN IS WORK—THE CLOTHING OF SPIRITS—
SPIRITS ARE INTERESTED IN OUR POLITICAL ELEC-
TIONS—CHURCHES—PLACES OF AMUSEMENT— EDU-
CATION OF CHILDREN.

The usual idea of heaven is rest.   The idea of "rest for the weary," is still prevalent in earth life : but each awakens to the great truth that heaven's rest is work—work in its highest sense.

Also the thought exists in many minds that heaven is freedom—and so it is to a disciplined spirit, for the interests of spirit life are so precious that such an one will, of his own free will, naturally gravitate toward that work most necessary to be done, while an undisciplined heart has to learn by degrees that the law must be fulfilled.

The temptation to describe to you my spirit home in some single chapter, grows stronger and stronger. Still I fear that in delineating it in all its features, I may fail to throw over it that spiritual halo, always existing, though I would impress upon your minds that, like your earthly homes, it is a tangible thing. I will, however, if I decide to enter into the minutiæ endeavor to give to each idea that spiritual coloring which would disarm the most critical.

I have told you heaven is work, but still no busy hands are making our wardrobe, no tired ones cleanse them.   Do we always wear the same clothing? is often asked.   I will answer, no. For as the spirit grows, as its capacity for good enlarges, our raiment grows brighter. It changes in texture, and assumes beauties before unknown.

Dress in your life depends upon the state of the pocket; here, on the state of the soul. Therefore, it is not strange to us see a spirit clothed in the plainest garb, while even then the old body is being arrayed in the finest of satin. On the other hand, I have seen spirits here so gorgeously clothed that they looked like white, glittering forms. I have no words to describe the texture or its manufacture, for it comes just as naturally as the spirit body, and as I said, the increase in beauty of body is in proportion to the increase of soul-worth. The manner and fashion of dressing as in earth, we leave behind, save when we wish to appear to our earth friends in a natural way; then, from the elements we can extract from the clothing of those around, we are taught to clothe ourselves for the time being.

Also, in appearing to the clairvoyant's vision, we, are instructed to appear, if possible, in garbs which have a resemblance to what we wore there, the more readily to be recognized by old friends.

In this partial description of my life here, I am trying to give you an account of scenes and employments as they are on the plane of progression, I now occupy, while one year hence I may be able to enter into glories as yet unthought of by me.

In these homes we enjoy sweet communion with kindred, unalloyed by the cares of earth. Here those who left you, aged and wrinkled with a long life of hard work, are again in the prime of life. Old age is a garment worn out, and with weakness, sickness and care, is left in the past.

Not only have we homes for the enjoyment of all that homes ever meant, but we have associations and organizations, carried on under the strictest parliamentary rules, to devise means to develop those who come to us unripe ; also, to throw our influence over earthly associations, and cause them to do efficient work. We have places for gathering where all side issues are discussed.

We have our Spiritual Congress for our nation's interest, which by developing harmony and engendering a right spirit, is enabled to throw a greater influence over your earthly Congress. There are many impediments to our even partial control, but mighty minds are working with power, ten-fold greater than those in earth life, to help strengthen any moves in the right direction, and make them effective for the nation's good.

We not only watch most anxiously who is elected to office (and if we find him a sensitive, throw upon his mind ideas which shall enter into the great work) but we exert as strong an influence as possible to have those elected upon whom we can act. Those of other nations take the same interest in their own affairs.

We continue to have this interest till, in the law of eternal growth, these matters which now seem so important to us will then appear of less moment, and our dropped threads will be taken up by other hands which will come after us, and woven into a beautiful fabric for the benefit of those who still labor in earth life.

If spirit life was made up of people who loved to pursue the same course, it would soon grow so monotonous as to make the heart sigh for variety, but it is not so. The churchman loves to have some place for worship ; the pleasure seeker wishes to go to places for amusement: the enthusiast, some place in which to drink in the thoughts freely given by noble minds; the children must needs attend schools for their benefit.

But all these places provided for the education of the soul are made so beautiful that there can be no monotony.

There is ever before us the necessity of toning up the mind to its greatest capacity, well knowing that as fast as it is needed, our minds will broaden and grow eager to receive the heavenly lessons—lessons which mean help to those below us and the highest culture to ourselves.

With the children here, there is no rebellion about attending school, for to be educated in spirit life means no books with their medley of figures until the brain grows dizzy, but for each one some gentle guardian who slowly, as the soul can understand, causes it to drink from the fountain of knowledge. Every lesson is demonstrated by facts.

Though in earth life children are often taught in the most imperfect way, here no organ is developed at the risk of others ; no sacrifice is made to push them in certain directions : but with eternity before them there is no need of haste.

So a balance is kept up which is destined to pave the way for efficient work, and encourage those who must sooner or later, go through the same experience.

Question—If children are so well cared for in spirit life, people may say, why is it not better for them to die young ?

Answer—Your criticism is a natural one; but

should I go into the minutiæ of the thought, it would take much space. The meaning is this : earth life is a school of which children are often robbed by disease, resulting in death.

It is not better for them to come over young, although the contingency is so nobly provided for.

The law of spirit life is to take up whatever is dropped in earth life and perfect it. Much time is spent in perfecting that which is not the legitimate work of spirit life, if the law of earth life had been fulfilled.

Spirit-children's ideas of earth life are not as well defined as if they had had its experiences, and though often carried back to the parents or to other proper persons, they cannot do as efficient work as they otherwise would. I might give many other reasons, but I will not multiply words. I will only add. that to pass over in childhood is not to experience a growth, through darkness : and thus nature's design is not as well perfected by the transplanting.

SAMUEL BOWLES.

PAPER NINTH.

THE RELIGIONS OF EARTH.

SOME OF THEIR ERRORS—HOW EVEN CHURCH PEOPLE ARE DISAPPOINT-
ED—HE PROTESTS AGAINST A THEOLOGY WHICH SAYS, "YOU MUST NOT
REASON"—MONOMANICS HUNTING FOR JESUS—DEATH—BED REPENTANCE
OF NO AVAIL—WHAT THE GOOD SPIRITS TEACH ABOUT RELIGION.

Far be it from me to strike with a rude hand at any of the religious or educational institutions of the day. And seeing as I do daily, the mistakes a-rising therefrom, I cannot withold from using the pen in a strong appeal to the thinkers of earth life to know whither they are drifting.

I would not if I could, strike at the heart of the church and creed, but were it in my power would open widely;the shutters and let in the light. I know that the lives of many, even under the "droppings of the sanctuary" are impure. They maintain their position only to answer to the call of some sordid purpose, and from the teachings of the church, looking forward to some time when they shall have lived their earth lives nearly out, they will throw their sins on Jesus, and be forgiven.

Such a doctrine given out to a grasping world is pernicious. There is no forgiveness save that wrought out by the suffering of self, and where the sin is, there the suffering must be, as the dire result of the cause. And now as I have had some experience, I will tell you why I feel this utter repugnance to the idea taught on earth that no matter what the lives of people are, no matter what their sins may be, repentance will bring them forgiveness at the end of the route.

A few instances I have observed of the intense disappointment of even people who have been in the church almost all their lives, have awakened in my heart the desire to so inform others that they may build up hopes different from the olden ones of "all in Jesus!" I would not dim the glory of this man of sorrows: I would not have the world look with less awe upon a life that ended on the cross; nor would I, if I could, change the idea of following that example, which says, "As ye would that others should do unto you, do ye even so unto them ;" for so far as one can in a selfish world, do so it will be a discipline here.

But my greatest protest is against that theology which says to its hearers, "You must not reason, you must trust ; you must not inquire into the mysteries of the Most High ; you must put away from your mind all other thought of being saved except through the cross of Christ. "

I have seen those whose vision, dying, was opened to the spirit world, declare they saw the face of Jesus, and the watchers, with holy awe, would feel like bowing down to the great Presence, when really it was the face of some loving relative, holding out a hand of welcome which the departing one saw.

Much patience is required to bring that spirit into an acquaintance with the fact. The throne of God, the shining face of his Savior, are all the time being prayed for. Even the tenderest care of loved ones who have long been over, fails to satisfy the hunger of a false education.

The Catholic faith in some degree is true–that such spirits have to go through a sort of purgatory before they can enjoy the bliss of spirit life.

My heart is sad to think, if the old Book is followed in some things, why people do not take more closely to heart that passage which says, "God. who will render to every man according to his deeds." That would avert much of the disappointment. for then they would know, even though they hope they are forgiven, that the old stains must be wiped out by earnest work here.

I am told that there are spirits here who have for years been monomaniacs on the one question.

"Hunting for Jesus." And it is sad to see the disappointment of so many who come over here, expecting a literal fulfillment of the descriptions of heaven which the Bible presents.

I have often wished for an opportunity to give some little crumbs of knowledge on this subject. Had I studied into it more when in earth life, I might not have felt it so deeply now. I would not take away one comfort the church gives, but I would add more to it, and show that people must prepare for a natural heaven.

There are those who come over here, steeped in crime, who, because of the supposed agonies of death which would assail the body, and the agonies of fear which assailed the mind, were visited by those who tried to comfort them by repeating the words of Him, who when on the cross said, "To day thou shalt be with me in Paradise." And with the excitement and prayers they appeared to die happy.

"Thank God, they repented at last," is said by fervent voices. And the souls expecting to be with Jesus in Paradise, come over where they reject the comfort and help extended to every one who enters upon spirit life.

They knew their lives had been vile, but still they had heard so much of forgiveness that they feel as if some particular injustice had been done to them : and it sometimes takes us very long to raise them from a hell they have built by their earth lives. The steps which lean upward are so slow, their propensities to evil so great, it is so much easier to come back to earth and live wickedness over again than to rise. The whole tendency is downward. I have felt shocked that this great law is so true to itself, that what ye sow that shall ye reap.

I wish that no picture shall be overdrawn. I know by old experience that the idea many people entertain of Spiritualism, is that it gives the freest license; that to live as one pleases, to discard restraint, in fact, to let loose all the prominent propensities, and indulge in them, is the sum total of spiritual existence.

But not so. True Spiritualism promises nothing of the kind. It teaches in the highest sense, that man's works do follow him. It shows the soul that it must not expect to transgress one law of the moral or physical world and escape the recoil upon itself.

It teaches that the body should be the pure temple for the soul, and any abuses, any excesses, any inclination to degrade, will drag the soul down. It teaches that there can be no repentance effectual save through self-suffering, worked out by slow degrees, and even then the scar is left. It shows men that if life is, it is ever existent, and that the two properties, good and evil, are capable of growth but surely the growth of one is at the expense of the other. It shows that unbridled passions, impure lives, are the outgrowth of old conditions, but because tolerated, they cause their victims long hours of darkness and dispair.

Spiritualism builds no lofty churches, makes no display in the world. It teaches that each soul must be a law unto itself. It links together the material and the spiritual, showing that Nature is Divinity, and exists in a blade of grass or in the noblest soul.

I would say to every one, think, live rightly, keep

the body pure, and your soul will be corresponding-
ly better. Make every day count you higher in the
scale of goodness. Ask not others to believe, but
live a life so pure that they shall say, "Surely Heav-
en is near, and they do have communion with the
angels." And last, though not least of all, Spiritualism invites to learn this lesson—no dread of death.
Death is the friend that unbinds your chains. It
is the tender love of the Infinite that says, "Come
hither soul and enter on your higher work." To the
good and bad it is alike a friend when the body is
worn out. It gives the good, chances for higher
work, greater usefulness and greater happiness. And
it says to the vile, "Now you have a chance to work
out of the old conditions and place yourself where
you can grow."

So, dread not death, and complain not that this
knowledge is a detriment, for well might it enter
every heart and make it better, and show all people
that they cannot escape the consequences of an evil
life.   SAMUEL BOWLES.

PAPER TENTH.
THE LAW OF SPIRIT CONTROL. WHY ERRORS SOMETIMES OCCUR.

The law of spirit control is of such a character, so
mysterious in its workings, so powerful for good or
evil, that I feel I must write one chapter upon this
subject, no matter if I cannot explain it clearly to
the minds of all.

The undeveloped spirit, in order with any degree
of certainty to reach his friends, must have tangible

contact with the medium—a contact in which this spirit is trying to displace all other spirits, waiting closely around. For to one medium in your life there are probably thousands of spirits; and could those spirits all press upon this one medium, the influence would be so crushing that the medium would have hard work to live in the body.

But this pressure is in a measure diminished to the earthly medium by these spirits being obliged to act through a medium in spirit life. Spirits in this life are daily helping to bring out more mediums here to do our work. You on earth wonder why the control of spirits differs so at different times and why certain conditions are necessarily different with different mediums to insure any chance for a perfect message, or even an imperfect one. The medium acting in spirit is usually what your mediums in earth life call their controls.

A spirit not long here or passing out of the body, under adverse circumstances, may be dimly conscious that he or she is wanted to comfort earth friends. The spirit is kindly led to one of these spiritual post-offices, and finds waiting friends there. When under other circumstances, this spirit might see his friends clearly, and have his reasoning faculties perfect as in earth life, yet often, because the batteries by which the control connects the sitter's brain with that of the spirit are so strong, and his desire to comply with his friend's request so great, together with the pressure of the surroundings, the many other waiting spirits, anxious to reach their own friends, he is unable to give only broken, disjointed sentences; and when asked to give his name.

could no more do it than a person under the will of a mesmerizer, who wills that his subject shall not give his name.

I have seen spirits all aglow with pleasure, watching their earth friends come to a medium, hoping to hear from their loved ones. The spirits would prepare what they would communicate, and when the chance came, the experience was so strange, that they were struck dumb; and if they were questioned by the spirit control, would in many instance, answer in a way which would detract from, rather than show forth the truth.

The first experience in controlling a medium, or in acting upon the medium's control, is an experience looked upon by the denizens of spirit life as of great moment, for in that way the heavenly growth is much accelerated.

Again a spirit may, by continued trials, find it easy to control one medium, and on their earth friends going with high hopes to another, be unable to control the second medium. Much depends upon the sitter's ideas and aims in the matter. If the mind is tranquil, and calls simply for truth—for some little word from their loved ones, and is passive and content, the sitter opens the way for better control.

Another cause of failure is the impression and mental atmosphere the sitter throws upon the earthly medium, making her feel that "you may be honest but you will bear watching," shutting up her lips and heart for fear a stray idea may reach the medium's brain from her. Such people deserve to be disappointed : the love of their so-called dead cannot awaken in the heart, charity for the living medium.

There are other causes for weakness in spirit control. No one medium nor no one spirit control can meet the needs of all. There are certain elements in body and soul as far severed as the antipodes ; and still the law of opposites is used in developing mediums. There are reasons, when the earth medium is going through a process of renewal, (menstruation) why there should be no attempt to get messages. The medium always feels it, and if any are given, they are usually imperfect.

Atmospheric conditions, when it is damp and lowery, retard the action of the batteries through which we work, while a cloudy day, with full electric force in the air, is often as good as a bright day.

The law of control must be learned here. We have to look upon the machinery of the human brain as you would look on machinery of which you would learn in earth life. One more point: It is often disputed that old sages and those hundreds of years in spirit life, could approach earth life in its grossness closely enough to speak through the lips they claim to. They do not speak directly through the lips of a medium by actual contact. Yet, by their superior wisdom, they are enabled to have knowedege of those in earth life and their needs.

I can explain this best by supposing a telegraph wire thousands of miles long. When a thought touches the further end, at each station on the way, that thought is reproduced, if the wires are rightly placed. Now we act by a system of refined telegraphy. A mind (some wise spirit) in the upper spheres with help, establishes a connection with a mind in earth life, (a medium) so that the thoughts which he sends to the medium's brain are thrown off the tongue.

A spiritual telegram is started in one of the upper spheres, far from contact with earth, and instead of stations along the line, are sensitives in the lower spirit spheres, upon whose minds the telegram strikes and gives these sensitives an impetus to speak the words, until perhaps millions of spirits have heard them, beside the small audience to whom they are addressed by the earthly agent.

Cherish and tone up mediumship, for it reaches from the highest heaven to the lowest hell, and teaches all, the necessity of studying the law of control.

Quest. What do you mean by pressure of surroundings?

Ans. The pressure of surroundings is first, the waiting spirits. Even though they may politely withdraw their minds, they are often busy establishing a connection sufficient to comply with the desires of their earth friends, even as a person in your life may kindly say, " I will not interfere, get your message first; yet his mind is active as to what he will ask when the opportunity comes.

Another cause of pressure is the shock felt when the magnetic power between them is established. The earth friend feels it in a degree if sensitive; but to the spirit it is as the rushing of mighty waters, because the shock is intensified and made more thrilling than the physical can take from any man-made electric battery.

Ques. How do you make your spiritual batteries?

Ans. We establish the sensation by currents in the air, made for our use, without the complicated machinery used by mortals.

Ques. Of what use is a name or question written in a folded paper or placed in a sealed envelope, or a lock of hair from the patient, as required by this medium?

Ans. The advantage gained is just what has been explained many times. The medium is often surrounded more or less by spirits who are trying to work upon her delicate organism, preparing for some opportunity to communicate with their friends. When a person, wishing a message, makes his appearance, the "controls" being busy when the call is made for that person's spirit friend to come, desire to get hold of some tangible request; and unless the spirit is called upon in a different way from the old one of father, mother, brother, wife, husband, &c, owing to the many desiring to reach their earth friends, though they may not be obtrusive, a confusion is produced.

But if the medium holds in her hand the direction to the spirit post-office, and thus gives the "control" the name of the spirit called for, it makes it much easier for him to help the spirit to communicate.

There are different laws established for different mediums and "controls." The fact that the sitter wishes to dictate and get messages in his own way is not only detrimental to successful control by the spirit, but often ends in throwing over the medium physical inability to work, and sometimes causing illness.

The lock of hair is required for this reason: Experienced spirit physicians have learned to trace through these delicate fibres the workings of the body. Every disease to which flesh is heir, leaves its impression on the hair, and being next to the brain, it is doubly susceptible to all which affects the body.

I may not have answered these questions as clearly as I ought, but I will say that so far as we are concerned, every question by the sitter could be sealed and sowed up in an envelope, but such a letter put into the hands of a medium, before the sitter, often throws this feeling over the medium: "He cannot trust me even in his own sight."

Mediums may in some cases, throw off this feeling, and we succeed, but there is left in the heart a feeling of heaviness. if not of grief, that she is an object of suspicion. The medium may feel the necessity and justice of this course, but still the idea will be entertained often that they are thought ill of.

SAMUEL BOWLES.

PAPER ELEVENTH.

SAMUEL BOWLES' SPIRIT HOME.

The idea prevalent among those of earth life of the eternal brotherhood of man over here, save in a general sense where one has indeed become a perfected spirit, is an erroneous one. Though peace and unity must prevail, yet it is not always that hearts beat in unison. It takes a long time for the spirit to throw off entirely the old dislikes. Although he may see where he has been in the wrong, yet the old error clings to him. Why should it not? The part of the man which hated is not dead. The death of the flesh cannot alter the thinking part save when by purity of action and learning to live rightly, these old tendences may be eliminated. Therefore, with this great variety of thought and action, it is certainly desirable that the spirit home should be so inhabited that there will be love, not hate.

In our homes on earth we loved at times to entertain friends, but after the confusion, how pleasant to have a few kindred hearts alone, aud have sweet communion. Therefore, the idea that every one is my brother, and here in spirit life has a right to enter my home and call it his, would be like being obliged to entertain company all of the time, or rather to have the sanctity of the home always broken.

Neither are people who by birth, having the same parents, always real brothers or sisters. By the force of ante-natal conditions they may be severed as far apart as the poles.

Therefore it would cause the most inharmonious conditions for them to reside together. In wisdom exceeding the wisdom of man, are our homes made up of those we can love the best, those with whom we can harmonize most completely. In every home there are rooms left vacant for the coming of loved ones, and loving hands adorn them and make them ready for those who seem nearest the portal, even as tender hearts have prompted hands to fashion the clinging ivy where rests the motionless form.

O! Love, thou art all of life worth living for, and all of immortality, because thou art infinite! No home in spirit life is over-crowded, and as all who are relatives cannot abide under one roof, there are often pleasant visits to friends here. It takes us only a moment to traverse distances which in earth life would be considered a great undertaking.

All our homes are not alike, but the purer and more worthy the spirit, the more beauty is prevalent all around. There are such different degrees of beauty needed to satisfy the different degrees of appreciation.

My spirit home is on a rise of ground back from the public path, surrounded by a beautiful green lawn, with the front nicely terraced. All around are lofty trees which give shade for resting places. A variety of garden chairs are placed where the best views can be obtained of mountain, lake and river. To the right of my home is a large flower garden where grow the beautiful soul parts of the flowers of earth. Lilies with their white petals almost transparent, roses with their vivid colorings, lilies of the valley nestled down among their green eaves, hyacinths, tube roses and verbenas, all blooming in unison, because they are not dependent on the season when they become spirit flowers.

The architecture of the house is not grand and imposing. It is a large, square mansion, with a wide hall in the middle; off from which are the rooms of the several occupants—rooms where we can have the strictest seclusion, and enjoy perfect repose—rooms where, if we wish, we can shut out the thoughts of our soul-work and sleep—not the sleep of the body, but to have curtains around the soul which gives us rest.

Our rooms are furnished much like yours there. Articles for convenience are all around : and to us there is a feeling of tangibility to everything, while to our eyes all these have that ethereal look which conveys to our minds the fact that we are surrounded by the soul of things.

But they supply our every need. About the home here, I have the same regularity that I had in earth life. There are hours for rest, hours for study hours for partaking of our food and hours in which we do the duties belonging to every soul—to raise the fallen and show undeveloped spirits, those taken out of the worst conditions in earth life how to rise, how to choose their spiritual homes and how to adorn them : for with souls who must redeem themselves, who are low and crude, the love of the beautiful is supplied step by step, according to their growth. But wherever we are, whatever our work, there is always a magnetic chord so strong that we can with one vibration, place ourselves where we can see the loved faces of earth life. Oh ! may the time come when it will be just as easy for us to communicate to them as it is to gaze into their loved faces and watch the workings of their minds.

I know I shall call down censure and ridicule in picturing a spirit home and a heaven so nearly like the earthly surroundings, but reason and common sense must teach you that if we exist as personalities, we must have some place in which to stay.

If you judge by your own earth life, you would not be satisfied always to mix with the motley crowd though it was in heaven. So has the All Power

ordained these things; and we, the children of an
everlasting Principle must work out the meaning of
our existence through eternity.

SAMUEL BOWLES.

PAPER TWELFTH.

In penning these papers, I am concious of the questions which may arise from my inability to give the
pen-pictures as I would wish. I know they lack that
conciseness and clearness which is necessary to carry conviction to the mind of the reader ; but when
I say I am doing the best I can, and striving in this
way to attain to a growth that will be a help in future efforts, I know that any fair-minded reader
will look to those parts which seem reasonable
to him, and compare the facts which I have stated
with the theories which are usually the outgrowth
of a false education.

If the heaven I picture is too natural and you
turn to the Book of books for a better description, ask yourselves which is the more reasonable?

Would not your feet tire, of walking on "solid
gold" and you turn gladly to nature's green carpet-
ing? And as to the musical part, would not a harp
express as much of materiality as a piano or organ?

It is the unrealness existing in minds there concerning the spirit world that I would battle with.
The impression that just as we find spirit life, just
so it will remain through all eternity, is another erroneous idea; for even the short time I have been
here, I find that every hour my spiritual vision awakens to new beauties.

Of course, these things existed on my entrance

here, but the time for me to enter into the enjoyment of them had not come. The tastes and dispositions remain the same as there, only as that which is impure is gradually left behind.

A grasping man will not be content unless he can continue to be grasping for those things he loved. Those coming here with strong inventive genius are encouraged in it, and through the influence of them, many of the wonderful pieces of mechanism are constructed on the earth plane.

All that can be done to lighten labor for those in earth life and to bring to light latent genius is done by those in spirit life. An artist in earth life will attract an artist spirit here, who will, by attaching himself by magnetic sympathy, in a measure realize again his earthly ambitions. But I am told this only exists for a time; that the old masters soon find such facilities for realizing their ambitions here that they leave the past and become engrossed in the great field for study before them.

Thus I think the idea which some mediums have that their controls are some of the ancients, and always with them, should be corrected. These advanced spirits would not have the inclination to attach themselves so closely to one in earth life. Yet by use of magnetic connection alluded to before, they may at times give help to the medium who is susceptible to refined influences. The highest minds may come in rapport with those in earth life through a medium having the proper inherent requisites. And thus the plans of those, wise and pure, may be worked out on the earth plane.

Ques—What is your house made of, and who made it?

Ans—You ask what is my house made of? To a mind surrounded by the material, this is very hard to make plain.   For ages on the earth plane there have been mansions built and houses of less pretentious appearance, but after doing good service there, they rot and crumble away.   This is because the subtle essence, which held the material together has departed, and as matter is ever existent, the finest part, instead of settling into the earth, must rise.

Therefore that essence as well as that which comes from buildings destroyed by fire, is fashioned by the All Creative Power into our homes.   And thus are homes made which cannot fail in their variety to please the most critical taste.

No spirit in a material sense, builds his home; still as the spirit expands, and his love for the beautiful is increased, the home he lives in will assume more beauty and be capable of changes until the spirit passes to a higher sphere.

Ques—What is the green grass made of, and does it go to seed?

Ans—When you wish me to tell you of what green grass is made, as with every other spiritual element you give me a question I cannot answer.   If I asked of what your grass is made, you would name the different properties existing, while I should have to say that our grass consists of the spirit of the properties of earthly grass.   Our grass is subject to changes.   In some instances I have seen it present the appearance of going to seed.   But that was not in contact with our homes, as it is the will of the owner that all should be beautiful here.   Our tastes are much the same as in earth life, but we work more with our will power than with our hands.

Ques—You wrote of cool shade trees. Do you have hot and cold weather there?

Ans—I wrote of cool shade, not so much because there is exceeding heat to flee from, as that the green shade is pleasant after the glare of light that exists. Though we have neither very hot nor very cold weather, still there is a variety which makes it pleasant for all. What would be agreeable for one might not be for another, and therefore climates are so well chosen and arranged that all may be satisfied.

Ques—If you have a variety of temperatures, how can flowers of different seasons in earth life, bloom together in spirit life?

Ans—As to the flowers all blooming together, your earth world, with its variations of climate, warm in some places, cold in others, is all the time producing for us the essence or spirit of the finest and most hardy flowers to go on with their eternal growth. Thus you see, when flowers once exist here, they always will exist; only subject to changes somewhat like the changes you have there.

I know this will be enigmatical to you, but see the wisdom of it. If one particular flower kept the same appearance, it would become monotonous, like those manufactured by hand in earth life. But it is not so. New buds and blossoms greet our sight—the old ones with their drooping heads, sending their spirit to the new.

Ques—How far is your home from earth, and in what sphere is it?

Ans—Counting by miles, I must be very many of

them from the earth, but by magnetic attraction and our power of locomotion, I am but little ways from the earth, for in an instant I am able to reach down when love calls me.

The spheres, as I have studied them, I wish to make the subject of a work hereafter, as I know with what little I have experienced, I shall give a somewhat different idea of them from what I perceive is in many minds in earth life. But in these papers, writing as I do with only a short experience, I wish to describe scenes from the plane on which I am now existing, and from that which I have passed through. I must, step by step, learn the glories that will open to me, and then tell you. In this effort I trust I have only begun a series of efforts which may grow clearer as I advance.

May all things be made plain to me, because I still would labor for my fellow-men—those who soon, at the longest, are to come over here and see whether my pen-pictures have led them into wrong ideas of spirit life.

Ques—You write in one place that you have no night there, yet you write in this paper of the glare of light. Do you have a glare all of the time? If not, what succeeds it?

Ans—I have previously stated that there is no night here, or no night like your night, but that each soul had its time for rest; and in order to rest, the conditions necessary must exist. As to the glare of light, I would state that different degrees of light and heat are necessary to the spiritual vegetation ever existent, and that as in earth life, we, when the light is most intense, seek for shade. As nature is

ever repeating itself, we find the most exquisite bow-
ers, with green foliage all around, where we can enjoy as much of the cooling breeze as though in earth
life we had come heated and weary to one of nature's
green recesses.

SAMUEL BOWLES.

PAPER THIRTEENTH.
THE SPIRITUAL CONGRESS.
HOW INTEMPERANCE IS TO BE OVERCOME.

When I promised to write on our spiritual congress, I perhaps gave the idea of describing a congress on the same plan with the earthly one, but this
is not really my design. I have before said that there
are no laws needed here, for in a truly spiritual life
every one is a law unto himself.

Real affairs of state are here not a necessity. If
spirit life made us selfish, the questions of the old,
struggling life might remain always behind. But
not so: while earth life is constantly sending over
such men as Horace Greeley, Charles Sumner, Wil-
liam H. Seward and hosts of similar noble men and
women, there will always remain workers for the nation. The old republic, so well loved, could not
meet with so much to pull it down, and not awaken in
hearts a desire to give it substantial aid, and blot forever from its pages the results of attempted dangerous innovations. Some of the very men mentioned
above can look back to times when they put forth
all their power to prevent the enactment of a law
because somewhere under the shelter of the proposed
law there might come a chance for self-aggrandizement.

Human nature is selfish; and he who conquers self most should be crowned king of himself. Here selfishness is gradually laid aside. Gold, the curse as well as the blessing of earth life, is not the coin used here. It will be remembered that all kinds of people are constantly coming to spirit life. Southern as well as northern politicians come with all their prejudices strongly fixed. Therefore it has been deemed desirable to have different places for gathering for the intelligent discussion of questions which in earth life were thought so momentous, and which were too apt to be viewed from one side only.

It has been my lot to be introduced into some of these gatherings, where questions are to be discussed preparatory to entering into our spiritual Congress.

I was struck with the cool, concise way in which all questions were treated—no thought of anger, no appearance of one setting his opinion above others, but a close reasoning and weighing of all questions which are of moment.

If a person sees that an argument, clothed with reason, is really above his former view of the question, there is a nobility of character shown in declaring himself vanquished. Remember, money for themselves cannot come of it; honor, by being in opposition, cannot come. Thus these questions are looked at in the right spirit and studied with a view of helping those in earth life who are making laws for the thousands who are to obey them. It is not an idea at all unreasonable to us that, in the near future the voices of departed statesmen may be heard again in the Senate and House of your Congress.

The spirit world, in its political phases is becoming awakened to the necessity of having something done to give any part of the national workings a semblance of the purity of the olden time. Men like Patrick Henry look blushingly on what used to be their pride.

Politics is such a dangerous maelstrom that when once a man is engulfed, there seems to be small chance of his escape, still retaining his purity of principle. The making of laws that are best for a struggling nation is left in the background. In order to reach the ears of these noble men, men too often surrounded by the fumes of liquor and tobacco, there must be such an amount of red tape that the applicant finds his pockets empty and his mind in such a confused whirl as to render him unable to give clearness to his ideas. Too often he departs feeling his one attempt for the protection of his fellowmen must be given up.

Viewing this mighty public machinery as you do, it may seem grand and imposing; but viewing the rottenness of heart, the flimsiness of principle, the power of gold; seeing men outside these places watching for some chance to buy or sell fellow men, watching women who too often degrade and themselves to help carry some point for which they will receive their reward in money, we feel the time has come to put into our work here such power as will strike out of existence some of the blots and canker spots marring the original beauty of the nation's escutcheon,

Therefore the necessity not only of a spiritual congress but of gatherings of all kinds whereby we can gain power to act on the worldly congress.

In our spiritual congress there convene those from every part of the nation who, through some past bond of sympathy with those who act in the earthly congress, may hope to awaken in them a desire to work for the real good of a great people.

Men who passed out of your life, with whitened heads, made so from their anxiety lest, by some inadvertence they might make mistakes, now almost groan in pain to see the carelessness with which a nation's honor is now held by a people living altogether too fast.

Our questions are not the questions that may be under immediate consideration in your congress, but those whereby we can establish the closest connection with those of you, destined to make the laws, and our best way to clear such heads of selfishness and the desire to be popular, long enough for them to seriously think whither they are letting the good old ship of state drift. For to our clear vision, it appears that with the facilities which the present time affords, and under the right management, laws might be so made and enforced, and the distribution of labor so equalized that there need not be a suffering family in the land where there are ten now.

When the laws which the spiritual congress would influence the earthly one to enact are in force, the power of King Alcohol shall be taken away, because we shall convince people that a law should be made against its manufacture, and also against its importation.

But some raise their voices, even here, and say that law would be incompatible with true liberty and a free country. The answer is, nothing is essential to liberty that makes chains, and where will you find stronger chains than those made by the demon, drink? You might say such a law would be an injury to the tillers of the soil, fruit raisers, &c. who depend on this traffic to make their sales.

We reply that for all we would take from the working world, we would restore tenfold. We would show you how little in all directions you really need, by the side of what you use, and also that with the wants of the body simplified, and by living nearer to nature, you will gain capacities for pure enjoyment never before acquired.

So now, all thinking ones in earth life, under whose observation these imperfect pages may come, lend us your aid, not only in living rightly and sending a good feeling that others shall understand, but when in the solitude of your home life, send up your earnest prayers to angel friends that they may help the upper congress to have such power over your nation's congress there, that the evils which surround you may gradually, by clean hands and pure hearts, be wiped from the nation's history, and that men shall be chosen for the earthly congress who may be in such harmony with higher powers that the way shall be made easier for the spiritual congress to work out its designs on the earthly congress.

SAMUEL BOWLES.

PAPER FOURTEENTH.
HOW TO HELP OUR LOVED ONES DIE.

Knowing as I do that I shall cause opposition, ridicule and perhaps trouble to the instrument through whom I write, I would like if possible, to throw over this work the garb of common sense, so that the most critical and unbelieving in spirit return will find something worthy of their attention, to whatever origin they ascribe it.

I have heretofore endeavored to analyze as I saw best, questions that had the greatest bearing on the needs of the day; and if I have been harsh, it was not meant. If I have sent you into a new path, though but for an instant, I pray it may be for your good.

I have touched more lightly on the social evils of the day than I shall when once I have a control perfect enough to give to the world that feeling with which I would inspire them—that of stopping now and thinking whether they have in their own homes a foundation strong and beautiful for the future of those to whom they give life.

I have been requested to give my ideal of a perfect reform in the social system, but it would be impossible for me while the real is the cause of such depressing thought and work. It would be like throwing seed on an ungrateful soil. Therefore, because I cannot handle it in all its bearings, and because there is in your land sickness which is daily leading to the change to life-everlasting, I would like to give you some of my ideas, grown strong by a short experience, of how to help your loved ones die. To you it may seem cruel.

Knowing how much depends on our state when we enter here, we deem it highly important, if the earth world will call change, death, that they learn how to die. There has been implanted in most humans the seeds of disease which rapidly developed by the lives they live, is the motive power wh brings them prematurely to spirit life.

This cause, which is ultimately to produce a natural effect, has seasons in which it seems to be nearly ready to consummate its purpose: but there comes some counter-irritant or some cause stronger, that for a time deadens the effect of this latent force, and the patient again rises from the sick bed. But each time this struggle happens, the power of the system to throw off this disease becomes weakened, and one notch lower in its bodily strength.

Much depends on the manner of living, the food eaten, the employment and all that goes to make up life, whether the body can still generate sufficient force after these attacks which come by heredity. But at the best, the will-power and the bodily-force must after a while bend to the inevitable.

Sooner or later the shell must give up its hold on the spirit. There are some pure lives, with antenatal conditions which, either from design or chance were nearly perfect, that fade away rather than sicken, and as the body, worn in all parts, gives way to the spiritual, which is intensified, angels catch glimpses of birth into spirit life which give them joy and arouses in their hearts stronger desires to throw such an influence over the earthly life that all people will be born right in order that they may die right, or rather enter the second birth.

But these instances are rare. The cases of inherited disease are so frequent that we wish to say to those who perceive the venom coursing through veins to its deadly work, and though vanquished, to take hold with a surer grip, you have a work to do.

When you see the utter hopelessness of the case

instead of letting the sad tears flow, show your bravery of spirit by striving to conquer yourselves. There before you is a loved one waiting the change. Disease at times, almost sways the spirit out of the body, but the clinging of home friends and the dread of entering an untried future has the effect for a time, to stay the power of disease.

Hopes are revived, and after prolonged suffering which need not have been, that spirit is released from the earthly body by the help of waiting angels.

Now how much better it would be if people would learn how to help each other die. When it is seen that earth life cannot long last, those waiting around the sick bed should speak cheeringly to the sufferer, of the beauties just out of sight. Instead of the sufferer catching sobs and looks of anguish for the last memory, he should see peaceful faces, and know that his loved ones are so sure, they can trust him and his waiting guardians out into a beautiful future.

Instead of holding your friends back with all the force of your will-power, you should say it is time for them to rest, and gently release the hold of your will, so they may not, in going forward, give backward glances of pity.

O! professed Christians! with a faith in the blood which cleanses from all sin—O! Spiritualists! feeling you are a step higher on the ladder of progression, you make that which nature intended as the final crowning of an earthly existence, the wading through a sea of tears. Remember that the prayer of spirit friends is, that men and women may be born right, then that they should die right, or enter upon spirit life without a fear. SAMUEL BOWLES.

PAPER FIFTEENTH.

HOW TO DEVELOP MEDIUMS.

I have before written of the necessity of pure, true channels through whom we can work. I have written of the necessity for the best ones. And now with the fact plainly before me that mediumship is in the future more than in the past, to be the great teacher for the uneducated millions, I see more and more necessity for the highest, purest development.

I would not wish to make an assertion incompatible with reason, for I know the usual idea is, " mediums are born, not made. " But seeing as I do in almost every organism the elements through which we could work, if those elements could be perfected, I am anxious that this truth may be so well understood that in the near future, there may be in nearly every family at least one through whom the spirits can work, and that there shall come to all, the happy and the sorrowful, that peace which may be given by our aid.

How to develop mediums has been a subject of much study, not only by me, but by many others, wiser than I. We have come to the conclusion that childhood is the best time in which to bring out these qualities. I would say to all who may read these lines, that as some prize the " family altar, " would we have you prize those times when, with your united family, you can sit around a table, with hands gently touching, and in the twilight of the room. raise your hearts in prayer to the angel world that some of the workers there may descend and take even the best, most beloved of your flock, for a medium in their cause. Let their be no levity, but gentle music and holy thoughts. Not that any feeling of awe need be attached to it, but have it implanted in the hearts of your children that loved ones may come, and greet the most tiny rap with as much gladness as you would the rap at the door which signalled the coming of a dear friend.

This subject, the beautiful harbinger of glad tidings, is not treated by believers with enough thought and reverence. Remember, it has opened a door for you that nothing else could, and it should be revered and loved because it is a part of God, a part of the All-Wise plan—a bridge over the gulf of death. Therefore would you have your children developed, it is almost like following in the footsteps of him who bore the cross up the mountain.

As the best mediums, through whom the most efficient work can be done, are the best people, it is highly necessary that each one should be grounded in morality, and from whose untarnished lives shall shine such truth that the most critical will say "If my loved ones can come back, I would like to have them come through such an one, who though bearing the cross of mediumship, hold their souls high above the filth which sometimes tarnishes the characters of sensitives through lack of will-power and proper training.

If the main object is to have good people developed into good mediums, and a chance is given in homes, by sitting regularly twice a week, but not over an hour at a time, but sitting that hour whether any result is obtained or not, by frequently invoking the presence of your spirit friends, by living

pure lives, by eating the most simple and nutritious
food, fish and cereals being more productive of good
than heavier meats, by keeping the system free from
all stimulants, even tea and coffee, by not vexing
your minds with dissensions and conflicts of the
day, you will give the most assistance to us, who
will gladly recognize all willingness to be one
of our aids.   I cannot enter into this subject as I
wish, for lack of time and space, but I trust I may
soon be enabled to give minute directions, after
having more thoroughly consulted those in whom I
have confidence, from their long experience here.

I also hope to put before that world I loved, such
proof that no reasonable person may doubt that these
papers come from me.   If I have failed in any part
of this work, to give definite ideas, I trust you will
look at the difficulties under which I labor, and thus
by extending your kindest feeling and a little of the
friendship of old, enable me to so perfect my control that what may come to you in the future, will
at least teach some the fact of continued existence.

I have taken up the pen with no desire for the
praises of men, but hoping to drop some words which
will enter the lives and hearts of those who, on the
great sea of uncertainty concerning their future, seek
some port from which to be able to judge honestly
the relations of life and death and the reasonable-
ness of a natural heaven.

SAMUEL BOWLES.

THE HYMNAL.

A practical Song Book for Congregational Singing.

This book of 75 pages contains 290 hymns (without music) most of which can be sung by a congregation. The tunes are easy and generally well-known. On the fly leaf are printed the titles and addresses of publishers of books containing the music. This music is mostly to be found in the Gospel Hymns and Spiritual Harp.

The words of this edition of the Hymnal are specially adapted for use in meetings of Spiritualists but other societies could use them. This edition contains 47 more hymns than the former edition, but these are added to the back part, and the old edition can be used with the new one.

The work is published and for sale by the Star Publishing Company at 91 Sherman street, Springfield, Mass, and can be supplied to societies for $14.00 per hundred copies: $8.00 for 50 copies: $4.50 for 25 copies: 20 cents per copy for a less number, postage, 3 cents a copy. Sample copies 23 cents, post paid.

The above prices apply to single orders. An order for 50 copies followed by another order for 50 copies a short time after will be filled at $8.00 each. Cash should accompany the order. Postage stamps accepted for sample copies.

☞ The Hymnal is by far the best and cheapest book of hymns yet issued for congregational singing.

www.ingramcontent.com/pod-product-compliance
Lightning Source LLC
Chambersburg PA
CBHW031243260626
47169CB00007B/2432